Rhino Wants a Wife

By Lucy Baker

First Published in the UK September 2016 by FBS Publishing Ltd.
22 Dereham Road, Thetford,
Norfolk. IP25 6ER
ISBN 978-0-9932043-5-7

A CIP catalogue record for this book is available from the British Library.

Cover design by Robin Dimond
Text Edited by Alasdair McKenzie
Typesetting by Scott Burditt

Paper stock used is natural, recyclable and made from wood grown in sustainable forests. The manufacturing processes conform to environmental regulations.

Rhino Wants a Wife

By Lucy Baker

FBS

Fabulous BookS

www.fbs-publishing.co.uk

Dedication

For Chris, my Rhino.

Rhino lived in the heart of the jungle,
surrounded by his animal friends.

He spent his days wallowing in muddy ditches and munching on delicious green plants. In many ways he was the happiest rhino that had ever lived, but there was one thing missing.

Rhino wanted a wife. A companion. Someone to wallow in muddy ditches with. Someone to munch on delicious green plants with.

The only trouble was, Rhino didn't know where he could find his perfect wife, or what she would be like. After some thought, he decided that he must set off on a journey to find a wife.

He was determined that he would not spend another day alone, so off he trudged.

Now, what Rhino didn't see was his cheekiest friend, Monkey, skipping along behind him, ready to make mischief ...

First, Rhino reached a dark thicket of undergrowth, where he saw Snake slinking round a tree trunk.

'Morning, Snake!' said Rhino cheerily. 'I'm looking for a wife, and I need some advice. Who would make the perfect wife?'

Snake flicked his tongue for a moment in thought before he replied, 'Well ... the perfect wife must slither and slide with a flexible body like rope. She must have a long wiggling tongue, a loud rattling tail and a hiss as she slides down a slope.'

'Great!' said Rhino, and off he went to find a wife.

Next, he reached some wide open scrubland, where he saw Giraffe nibbling twigs in the treetops.

'Hello, Giraffe!' said Rhino cheerily. 'I'm looking for a wife, and I need some advice. Who would make the perfect wife?'

Giraffe tapped his hooves thoughtfully before he replied,

'Well ... the perfect wife
must be as tall as a tower,
with a neck that is graceful
and lean. She must have
a calm, gentle nature,
fluttering lashes and a gallop
that is swift and serene.'

'Great!' said Rhino, and off
he went to find a wife.

As Rhino headed off, Monkey swung down from a twisted vine and cackled with glee. He imagined what kind of extraordinary creature would have a `slithering body' and a 'tall neck'. He knew Rhino would have a difficult job finding a wife like that! That gave Monkey the naughtiest of naughty ideas, and he grabbed a long, gnarly stick ...

Meanwhile, Rhino had reached a forest clearing showered in sunlight, where he saw Parrot perched on a branch.

'Good day, Parrot!' said Rhino cheerily. 'I'm looking for a wife, and I need some advice. Who would make the perfect wife?'

Parrot clicked his beak and ruffled his glorious feathers in thought before answering, 'Well ... the perfect wife must chatter, natter and squawk, she should sing, whistle, twitter and mutter. She must have bright, vibrant feathers, sharp clasping claws and set my heart all of a flutter.'

'Great!' said Rhino, and
off he went to find a wife.

Sniggering, Monkey started practising his
best squawking sounds ...

Soon after, Rhino found himself
on a swampy river bank, where
he saw Crocodile wading
through the cool water.

'Hi, Crocodile!' said Rhino
cheerily. 'I'm looking for a wife,
and I need some advice. Who
would make the perfect wife?'

Crocodile thrashed his tail wildly as he pondered, and replied, 'Well ... the perfect wife must have an enormous toothy grin, and find meat simply delicious. She should have ridged, scaly skin, beady black eyes and be fantastically snappy and vicious.'

'Great!' said Rhino, and off he went to find a wife.

Immediately, Monkey started to perfect his evil stare and ferocious toothy grin. He scooped up a handful of lily pads from the water as he dashed off after Rhino.

What could he be up to?

In the afternoon, Rhino made his way towards the leafy jungle bushes, where he saw Sloth snoozing peacefully on a branch.

'Good afternoon, Sloth!' said Rhino cheerily. 'I'm looking for a wife, and I need some advice. Who would make the perfect wife?'

Sloth yawned idly before saying,
'Well ... the perfect wife must be
quiet and lazy, and sleep with a
whistling snore. She must have
soft, silky fur, dingle dangle all day
and be the most terrible bore.'

'Great!' said Rhino, and off
he went to find a wife.

Just as Sloth was about to return to his slumber, he felt an enormous tug on his bottom which made him yell out in pain. As he turned around, all he could see was a curly, brown tail disappearing into the jungle.

He looked down at his sore behind
and couldn't believe his sleepy eyes
when he saw a patch of pink skin
where his fur should be ...

Finally, Rhino collapsed, exhausted after his journey. Suddenly, he saw Stick Insect rustling among the leaves on the forest floor (he nearly sat on him, after all, he did look awfully like a real stick ...).

'Nice to see you Stick Insect!' said Rhino cheerily. 'I'm looking for a wife, and I need some advice.'

'Who would make the perfect wife?'

Stick Insect crawled speedily towards Rhino before whispering in a small voice, 'Well ... the perfect wife must be the dullest of brown, with a body the tiniest of tiny. She must skitter and scamper and hide in the trees with a body so twig-like, it's spiny.'

'Great!' said Rhino, and off he went (again) to find a wife, unaware that a trouble-making monkey was just footsteps behind ...

As Rhino plodded slowly towards his favourite tree, he thought about all the advice his friends had given him.

So ... he was looking for a wife that would slither and gallop and be both scaly and furry?

Sloth said she should be a bore, but Crocodile said she should be vicious?

'Hang on,' thought Rhino. 'Giraffe said the perfect wife would be as tall as a tower, but Stick Insect said she should be the tiniest of tiny?!'

Monkey watched on as he saw Rhino grow more and more confused by the different advice he had heard from his friends.

'Just as I hoped!' giggled Monkey as he began to put his cheeky plan into action.

Still puzzling over what his friends had said, Rhino looked up and saw an even more puzzling sight. What kind of creature was this?

Big, round green scales, a toothy grin, spiny legs, a long neck, slithering on its tummy towards him as it squawked strangely.

It even had a patch of silky fur!

This must be the perfect wife for me! Excited, Rhino scrambled to his feet and lumbered towards this fascinating creature. It didn't feel exactly as he expected. He wanted the excited feeling Mr Butterfly had once told him about. 'Maybe that will come later?' he thought.

Just as Rhino was about to speak to the perfect wife, a huge gust of wind swept over the jungle and the perfect wife began to disappear.

Rhino watched as the scales floated away, spiny legs fell off and fur went drifting into the distance. When the wind settled, all that was left was a shifty-looking monkey clasping a long stick and chuckling ...

'I fooled you, I fooled you!' he cried as he scampered away towards the trees.

Even though his cheeky friend had teased him, it made Rhino think. The jumbly jungle wife that Monkey had invented had made him realise that everyone must have a slightly different version of what is perfect. Rhino smiled. Maybe his idea of the perfect wife would be different to that of his friends?

As he sat and thought, he looked over towards his favourite muddy ditch and saw a silhouette of someone nearby. He looked more closely and realised that ...

... she was great and galumphing, her body was wrinkled and fat. She had a stupendous horn, thick stomping legs and her feet were like plates, round and flat.

Rhino's heart felt warm. He was sure that this time he had really seen his perfect wife.

She wasn't hissing. She wasn't fluttering her lashes. She wasn't squawking, snapping, snoozing or skittering, but to him, she was perfect.

Rhino was filled with happiness from top to toe. He knew that there was someone perfect for everyone ...

... perhaps even mischievous monkeys?

About the Author

Lucy grew up in rural Buckinghamshire in a house nicknamed the 'Bakerzoo'. With dozens of pets, three younger sisters and actors for parents, her childhood was never dull.

After completing a degree in Criminology and working as a television researcher, Lucy decided to become and remains a primary school teacher. She loves to read books to her class to inspire them to create and write their own stories.

www.lucybakerbooks.com
www.fbs-publishing.co.uk

Lightning Source UK Ltd.
Milton Keynes UK
UKRC02n0401130916
282850UK00007B/26
* 9 7 8 0 9 9 3 2 0 4 3 5 7 *